I Am Goose!

Dorothia Rohner

Illustrated by Vanya Nastanlieva

CLARION BOOKS
Houghton Mifflin Harcourt
Boston   New York

We're gonna need more popcorn!

Oh yeah!

Extra butter this time.

With a loving and grateful heart—for Homer and the many years of
encouragement, patience, and support for my creative muses.
—D.R.

For my sister, with love
—V.N.

Clarion Books, 3 Park Avenue, New York, New York 10016
Text copyright © 2020 by Dorothia Rohner, Illustrations copyright © 2020 by Vanya Nastanlieva
All rights reserved. For information about permission to reproduce selections from this book, write to trade.permissions@hmhco.com or
to Permissions, Houghton Mifflin Harcourt Publishing Company, 3 Park Avenue, 19th Floor, New York, New York 10016.
Clarion Books is an imprint of Houghton Mifflin Harcourt Publishing Company.

hmhbooks.com

The illustrations in this book were done in mixed media. The text was set in P22 Garamouche and Aunt Mildred MVP.

Library of Congress Cataloging-in-Publication Data
Names: Rohner, Dorothia, author. | Nastanlieva, Vanya, illustrator.
Title: I am goose! / Dorothia Rohner ; illustrated by Vanya Nastanlieva.
Description: Boston ; New York : Clarion Books, Houghton Mifflin Harcourt, [2020] | Summary: Goose asks to play "Duck, Duck,
Goose" with the other animals and birds, but causes trouble by insisting that none of them can possibly be goose.
Identifiers: LCCN 2018051999 | ISBN 9781328841599 (hardcover picture book)
Subjects: | CYAC: Games—Fiction. | Geese—Fiction. | Animals—Fiction. | Birds—Fiction. | Humorous stories.
Classification: LCC PZ7.1.R6645 Iaah 2020 | DDC [E]—dc23
LC record available at https://lccn.loc.gov/2018051999

Manufactured in China
SCP 10 9 8 7 6 5 4 3 2 1
4500783584